2/11

Dear Parent:

Congratulations! Your child is taking the first steps on an exciting journey. The destination? Independent reading!

STEP INTO READING® will help your child get there. The program offers five steps to reading success. Each step includes fun stories and colorful art. There are also Step into Reading Sticker Books, Step into Reading Math Readers, Step into Reading Phonics Readers, Step into Reading Write-In Readers, and Step into Reading Phonics Boxed Sets—a complete literacy program with something to interest every child.

Learning to Read, Step by Step!

Ready to Read Preschool–Kindergarten
• big type and easy words • rhyme and rhythm • picture clues
For children who know the alphabet and are eager to begin reading.

Reading with Help Preschool–Grade 1
• basic vocabulary • short sentences • simple stories
For children who recognize familiar words and sound out new words with help.

Reading on Your Own Grades 1–3
• engaging characters • easy-to-follow plots • popular topics
For children who are ready to read on their own.

Reading Paragraphs Grades 2–3
• challenging vocabulary • short paragraphs • exciting stories
For newly independent readers who read simple sentences with confidence.

Ready for Chapters Grades 2–4
• chapters • longer paragraphs • full-color art
For children who want to take the plunge into chapter books but still like colorful pictures.

STEP INTO READING® is designed to give every child a successful reading experience. The grade levels are only guides. Children can progress through the steps at their own speed, developing confidence in their reading, no matter what their grade.

Remember, a lifetime love of reading starts with a single step!

For Lucy Rae
—M.L.

Materials and characters from the movie *Cars*. Copyright © 2006, 2011 Disney/Pixar.
Disney/Pixar elements © Disney/Pixar, not including underlying vehicles owned by third parties:
Fiat is a trademark of Fiat S.p.A.; Jeep® and the Jeep® grille design are registered trademarks
of Chrysler LLC. Mack is a registered trademark of Mack Trucks, Inc.; Mercury is a registered
trademark of Ford Motor Company; Sarge's rank insignia design used with the approval of the
U.S. Army. Volkswagen trademarks, design patents and copyrights are used with the approval
of the owner, Volkswagen AG. Background inspired by the Cadillac Ranch by Ant Farm (Lord,
Michels and Marquez) © 1974. All rights reserved. Published in the United States by Random
House Children's Books, a division of Random House, Inc., 1745 Broadway, New York, NY 10019,
and in Canada by Random House of Canada Limited, Toronto, in conjunction with Disney
Enterprises, Inc.

Step into Reading, Random House, and the Random House colophon are registered trademarks of
Random House, Inc.

Visit us on the Web!
StepIntoReading.com
www.randomhouse.com/kids

Educators and librarians, for a variety of teaching tools, visit us at
www.randomhouse.com/teachers

ISBN: 978-0-7364-2765-4 (trade)—ISBN: 978-0-7364-8091-8 (lib.bdg.)

Printed in the United States of America

10 9 8 7 6 5 4 3 2 1

DISNEY · PIXAR

Cars

PACIFIC FLYER

A113

A113

GO, GO, GO!

By Melissa Lagonegro
Illustrated by Ron Cohee, Art Mawhinney,
and the Disney Storybook Artists

Random House 🏠 New York

Everyone is
on the go
in Radiator Springs!

Lightning is
a race car.

He drives fast.

Mater is a tow truck.

He pulls cars

out of trouble.

Fillmore is a van.

He is green.

He makes fuel.

Mack is a trailer truck.

He carries Lightning.

Al Oft is a blimp.
He floats
in the sky.

Red is a fire truck.

He has a water hose.

Tractors have big wheels.

They tip over easily.

Sheriff is a police car.

He has a red light

and a siren.

Guido is a forklift.

He carries tires.

The helicopter flies
in the air.
Its blades spin
around and around!

Sarge is a 4x4.

He rides

over rocks.

Frank is a combine.

He cuts grain.

The train rides

on a track.

Bulldozers are big
and strong.

Go, go, go!